My Weirdest School #8

Mrs. Master Is a Disaster!

Dan Gutman

Pictures by
Jim Paillot

HARPER
An Imprint of HarperCollinsPublishers

To Keegan Masters

*Warning! Toilet jokes ahead. If you don't approve of
toilet jokes, don't read this book.
And get a sense of humor.*

My Weirdest School #8: Mrs. Master Is a Disaster!
Text copyright © 2017 by Dan Gutman
Illustrations copyright © 2017 by Jim Paillot

ISBN 978-0-06-242933-9 (pbk. bdg.)—ISBN 978-0-06-242934-6 (library bdg.)

Typography by Celeste Knudsen
17 18 19 20 21   OPM   10 9 8 7 6 5 4 3 2 1

❖

First Edition

Contents

Old Fogies and Young Fogies

My name is A.J. and I hate toilet seats.

Let me explain. On Saturday, my family was going to go to the movies to see *Star Wars*. But then the toilet seat in our bathroom broke. So we had to spend the whole day at the mall shopping for a new toilet seat. Bummer in the summer! That's why I hate toilet seats.

Okay, I promise there's nothing else in this book about toilet seats. Quick, look down!*

Anyway, when I got to the front steps at Ella Mentry School on Monday morning, the weirdest thing in the history of the world was going on. The place was swarming with old fogies! Men and ladies with canes and walkers and gray hair were *everywhere*.

"What's going on?" asked my friend Michael, who never ties his shoes.

"Did they turn the school into a retirement home?" asked Ryan, who will eat anything, even stuff that isn't food.

---

* Ha-ha! Made you look down! Nah-nah-nah boo-boo on you!

"Does this mean we don't have school anymore?" asked Neil, who we call the nude kid even though he wears clothes.

"NO MORE SCHOOL!" I chanted. "NO MORE SCHOOL! NO MORE SCHOOL!"

I figured everybody was going to start chanting "No more school!" with me. I looked around. Nobody else was chanting. Everybody was looking at me. I hate when that happens.

"What's with all the old fogies?" I asked.

"It's not nice to say 'old fogies,' Arlo," said Andrea Young, this annoying girl with curly brown hair. "Older people are called 'senior citizens.' Today is Grandparents Day, remember?"

"My grandma is coming in to talk about

her life," said Alexia, this girl who rides a skateboard all the time.

Oh, yeah. I forgot. My grandpa Bert told me he would be coming to school too.

We went inside and walked a million hundred miles to Mr. Cooper's class. Grandpa Bert and a bunch of other old fogies were lined up in the back of the room.

"Welcome to Grandparents Day," said

Mr. Cooper, after we pledged the allegiance. "I'm glad so many grandparents were able to join us today. We can learn a lot from listening to people who have lived longer than we have. Who would like their grandma or grandpa to go first?

"Me!" shouted Andrea.

"Me!" shouted Andrea's crybaby friend, Emily.

"Me!" shouted Ryan.

In case you were wondering, everybody was shouting "Me!" But Mr. Cooper picked Grandpa Bert, so nah-nah-nah boo-boo on everybody else.

Grandpa Bert walked up to the front of the class.

"My name is Bert," he said. "I'm A.J.'s grandpa, and I'm an old fogy. So I guess that makes you kids *young* fogies."

Everybody laughed even though Grandpa Bert didn't say anything funny.

"Tell us a little bit about yourself, Bert," said Mr. Cooper.

"I'm just an old coot," said Grandpa Bert. "Are there any young coots? How come all coots are old? What's a coot anyway? And what's the difference between a coot and a fogy?"

"Uh, how old *are* you, Bert?" asked Mr. Cooper.

"I'm seventy years old," he replied.

"Gasp!" we all gasped. I can't imagine *ever* being seventy.

"Yep, that's pretty old," said Grandpa Bert. "I was born back in the 20th century."

"WOW," we all said, which is "MOM" upside down. It must have been weird to live in a different century. I bet everything was black and white when Grandpa Bert was young.

"I'm as old as some turtles," he said. "Hey,

maybe that's why turtles move so slowly. Because they're old. But come to think of it, even young turtles move slowly. Maybe turtles are just *born* old. Did you kids know that sea turtles can make a noise just like burping?"

Then he made some funny burping noises with his armpit. Grandpa Bert is weird.

"Okay, thank you, Bert," said Mr. Cooper. "How about Andrea's grandma? Would you like to go next?"

Andrea's grandma went to the front of the class. She was all dressed up like she was going to a wedding. She told us her name was Mrs. Young and that she used to be a teacher.

"Does anybody have a question for Mrs. Young?" asked Mr. Cooper.

"Did they have Froot Loops when you were a kid?" I asked.

"What's a Froot Loop?" asked Andrea's grandma.

"Gasp!" we all gasped. I can't imagine not knowing what Froot Loops are.

"Froot Loops are my favorite cereal," I told her. "They taste like candy, but they have the word 'fruit' in them so you know they're good for you."

"They sound disgusting," Andrea's grandma replied. "I don't approve of sugary foods."

"Did they have video games when you were a kid?" asked Neil.

"No," Mrs. Young replied. "When my friends and I wanted to play, we had to go outside."

"Outside?" I asked. "Where's *that*?"

Everybody laughed even though I didn't say anything funny.

One by one, the other old fogies came up and told us about their lives. Michael's grandfather was a soldier in the army. Emily's grandmother worked in a bank.

Neil's grandmother told us that when she was a teenager, she went to someplace called Woodstock. It must have been horrible, because she had to live outside in the mud for three days.

"Blah blah blah blah," all the old fogies told us. "Blah blah blah blah when I was your age blah blah blah blah the good old days blah blah blah blah."

The last of the old fogies was Alexia's grandmother Mrs. Master. She told us she was an inventor and that she started her own company.

"What did you invent?" asked Andrea.

"Oh, all kinds of things," Mrs. Master replied. "Shoes that tie themselves,

eyeglasses with built-in windshield wip-
ers. You know that rubber thing your
parents use when they can't take the lid
off of a jar?"

"You invented *that*?" we all asked.

"Yep," replied Mrs. Master. "*Somebody* had to. How else would we get the lids off of jars?"

It was really interesting listening to the old fogies talk about their lives. But it went on *all* morning. I thought that by the time the grandparents were finished, *I* might be a grandparent.

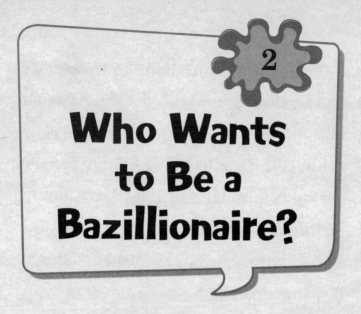

Who Wants to Be a Bazillionaire?

"Okay, it's time for spelling," Mr. Cooper said after all the old fogies were gone.

"Yay!" shouted all the girls.

"Boo!" shouted all the boys.

"Most words are easy to spell," Mr. Cooper told us. "You can just sound them out. Can somebody spell what Mr. Klutz's job is?"

Andrea waved her hand in the air like she was trying to signal a plane from a desert island. Mr. Cooper called on her, of course.

"Mr. Klutz is the P-R-I-N-C-I-P-L-E," guessed Andrea.

"That's close," said Mr. Cooper. "Remember, the principal is your *pal*."

"P-R-I-N-C-A-P-A-L," guessed Ryan.

"Nice try, but no," said Mr. Cooper. "Just sound it out."

"P-R-I-N-S-I-P-A-L," guessed Michael.

"No, sorry," said Mr. Cooper.

"P-R-I-N-S-I-P-L-E," guessed Emily.

Mr. Cooper slapped his own forehead. Grown-ups are always slapping their foreheads. Nobody knows why.

At that moment, the lunch bell rang.

"Yay!" everybody shouted as we grabbed our lunch bags and ran out the door. I guess we'll never learn the right way to spell what Mr. Klutz's job is.

We walked a million hundred miles to the vomitorium. I had a peanut butter and jelly sandwich. Ryan had a peanut butter and jelly sandwich too, but he turned his sandwich upside down and said it was a jelly and peanut butter sandwich. Ryan is weird.

"Wasn't Grandparents Day fun?" asked Emily.

"I hope I never get old," Michael said. "I don't want to be an old fogy."

"Or an old coot," I said.

"*Everybody* gets old, Arlo," said Andrea, who calls me by my real name because she knows I don't like it. "Getting old is part of life."

"Your grandmother was a cool lady, Alexia," said Emily. "I didn't know that she invented all those things."

"Yeah, she invented lots of stuff," said Alexia. "Last week she invented a cookie dunker that prevents your hand from getting full of milk when you dunk a cookie."

"I bet she made a ton of money," I said. "Hundreds of dollars."

"Thousands!" said Ryan.

"Millions!" said Neil.

"Bazillions!" said Michael.

I don't even know if "bazillions" is a real word. It sounds like a made-up number, if you ask me. But even if it is fake, Alexia's grandmother must be *really* rich.

"Hey, *we* should invent something and start our own company," I said. "Then *we* could make bazillions."

"A.J., you're a genius!" said Ryan.

I should get the Nobel Prize for that idea.*

Instead of going to recess after we finished lunch, we went to Mr. Klutz's office. When we got there, he was hanging upside down from a bar near the ceiling. He had on boots that were attached to the bar.

"What are you doing up there?" I asked.

"Oh, just hanging around," Mr. Klutz said as he pulled himself out of his boots and jumped down on the floor. "What can I do for you? This must be pretty important for you kids to miss recess."

---

* You probably think that's a prize they give out to people who don't have bells. But it's not! Where did you get that dumb idea?

"We want to start a company, like my grandma did," said Alexia.

"That's a great idea!" said Mr. Klutz. "I like my students to think big. What sort of company do you want to start?"

"We don't know," said Andrea.

"We should make something," said Ryan.

"Well, what do you want to make?" asked Mr. Klutz.

"We want to make *bazillions*!" I said.

"Hmmmmm," said Mr. Klutz. "I don't know if I can help you. I don't know the first thing about starting a company."

That's when I came up with *another* genius idea.

"Why don't you call your grandma on

the phone, Alexia?" I suggested. "Maybe she'll help us."

"That's a great idea!" Mr. Klutz said as he picked up his phone.

No wonder I'm in the gifted and talented program.

Alexia told Mr. Klutz the cell phone number for Mrs. Master, and he dialed it. It was like that TV show where they ask people questions, and if they can't answer them, they can call a friend. Mr. Klutz turned on the speaker on his phone so we could hear what Alexia's grandmother had to say.

"Hello?" said Mrs. Master.

"This is Mr. Klutz over at Ella Mentry

School," said Mr. Klutz. "May I speak with Mrs. Master?"

"Speaking," said Mrs. Master.

"You really inspired Alexia and her classmates this morning," said Mr. Klutz. "Now they want to start their own company. Can you give them any advice?"

"I'm pretty much retired now, so I have plenty of time," replied Mrs. Master. "I'll be right over."

"Yay!" we all shouted.

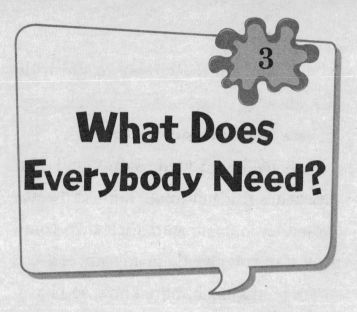

What Does Everybody Need?

We walked back to Mr. Cooper's class. When we got there, we told him that Mrs. Master was going to help us start our own company so we could make bazillions.

"You'll need to count all that money," Mr. Cooper said. "Math is very important in the business world. So let's all turn to page twenty-three in our math—"

He never got the chance to finish his sentence. At that moment, you'll never believe who came though the door.

Nobody! You can't come through a door. Doors are made of wood. But you'll never believe who came through the door*way*. It was Mrs. Master! And she was riding a hover board!

"Hello, my young fogies!" she hollered.

"Mrs. Master, why are you riding a hover board?" asked Mr. Cooper.

"Oh, it's not just a hover board," she said. "It's a combination hover board and *lawn mower*! So you can hover and mow at the same time. It's my latest invention."

"Cool!" we all shouted.

"Grandma is always coming up with

ideas like that," said Alexia.

"So you want to make an invention and start your own company," said Mrs. Master. "What do you want to invent?"

"Uh, we don't know, Grandma," admitted Alexia.

"Hmmm," said Mrs. Master. "Well, the first rule of inventing is to invent something that everybody needs."

"Let's put on our thinking caps," said Mr. Cooper.

I looked in my desk. There was no thinking cap in there. I would just have to think without one.

What does everybody need? I thought and thought. I was thinking so hard that my brain hurt.

"Food!" shouted Andrea. "Everybody needs food."

"Clothes!" shouted Neil the nude kid.

"Shelter!" shouted Ryan. "We all need a place to live."

"That's true," said Mrs. Master.

"Pencils," said Mr. Cooper. "I'm always losing my pencil."

Everybody was thinking. That's when I got the greatest idea in the history of the world.

"A toilet seat!" I shouted.

Everybody laughed even though I didn't say anything funny.

Okay, I *know* it said there wasn't going to be anything else in this book about toilet seats. But think about it—*everybody* needs a toilet seat. If you don't have a toilet seat, you'll fall into the toilet!

"You're right, A.J.," said Mr. Cooper.

"That's not a bad idea!"

"The only problem is that most people already *have* a toilet seat," said Mrs. Master. "When you buy a toilet, it comes with a seat. An inventor wants to invent something that people don't already have."

"What if we were to make the toilet seat *special*?" I said. "Or different."

"How can we make a toilet seat different?" asked Mr. Cooper. "Aren't all toilet seats pretty much the same?"

I thought and thought and thought some more. I thought my head was going to explode.

"What if the toilet seat was *heated*?" I asked. "Then it wouldn't feel cold when you sit on it."

"That's a good idea, A.J!" said Mr. Cooper. He looked really excited.

"Yeah!" everybody shouted.

"I think they *have* heated toilet seats," said Mrs. Master. "Somebody already invented it."

"Ohhh," everybody groaned.

"Hmmmm," said Mr. Cooper.

Grown-ups always say "Hmmmm" when they're thinking. Nobody knows why.

"How about a heated toilet seat that glows in the dark?" Mr. Cooper suggested. "Then you can find the toilet at night without turning the bathroom light on!"

"Yeah!" everybody shouted.

"Well, *that* would be different," said

Mrs. Master. "I don't think anybody ever invented that."

"And we can make the toilet seat scented, so it smells pretty," said Andrea.

"A heated, scented toilet seat that glows in the dark!" shouted Mr. Cooper. "I love this idea!"

"And we could make it talk!" I shouted.

Everybody laughed even though I didn't say anything funny.

"Arlo, why would *anybody* in the world want a talking toilet seat?" asked Andrea, rolling her eyes.

"Because it's lonely in the bathroom," I explained. "A talking toilet seat would help keep you company."

"It's brilliant!" shouted Mrs. Master.

"A.J., I think you're a genius!" shouted Mr. Cooper.

"We're gonna make *bazillions*!" shouted Michael.

It was the greatest moment of my life.

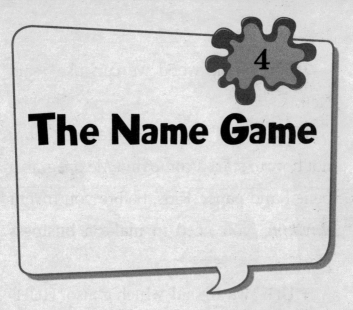

The Name Game

Everybody was excited about inventing the first heated, scented, talking toilet seat that glows in the dark. Even Mr. Cooper.

"I can't wait to get started!" he said, clapping his hands together. "I have a workshop in my basement. I can build it there tonight."

"I can bring over a hammer," said Ryan.

"I have some wood we can use," said Neil.

"Slow down!" said Mrs. Master. *"That's* not how to start a company! Alexia, grab a pencil and paper. Kids, before you invent *anything*, you need to make a business plan."

"HUH?" we all said, which is also "HUH" backward.

"You need to explain to the world why your company will be successful," said Mrs. Master. "Let me see. Does anybody know many houses there are in China?"

Andrea took out her smartphone. Her parents got her one so she could look stuff up and show everybody how smart she is.

"It says here that there are almost five

hundred million households in China," she reported.

"Good," said Mrs. Master. "Write that down, Alexia. And let's say that one out of every ten families in China bought our toilet seat. How many toilet seats would they buy?"

Andrea fooled around with her smartphone some more.

"Almost fifty *million* toilet seats!" Andrea said.

"WOW!" we all shouted, which is "MOM" upside down.

"Good," said Mrs. Master. "Alexia, write that down. Fifty million toilet seats."

"That's a lot of toilet seats!" said Emily.

"And that's just in China," said Mr.

Cooper. "The worldwide market will be much bigger."

"We're gonna make bazillions!" shouted Michael.

We worked on the business plan for the rest of the afternoon. Mr. Cooper didn't try to teach us spelling or math or any other boring stuff. All he cared about was the toilet seat.

It was almost three o'clock. For once in my life, I didn't want to leave school at the end of the day. Starting a company was fun!

"The next thing we need to think about is a name," said Mrs. Master.

"We already have names," I said. "My name is A.J."

"Not names for *us*, dumbhead!" said Andrea. "We need a name for the *toilet seat*!"

Why can't a truck full of toilet seats fall on Andrea's head? I was going to say something mean to her, but I was too busy trying to think of a good name for our toilet seat. I couldn't come up with anything.

"How about the Heated, Scented, Talking, Glow-in-the-Dark Toilet Seat?" suggested Alexia.

"That's a little wordy, dear," said Mrs. Master.

"It has to be a cool name," said Ryan. "Like . . . Cozy Crapper."

"'Crapper' is not a nice word," said Mrs. Master. "Nobody will buy a toilet seat with the word 'crapper' in its name."

"Why not?" Ryan asked. "The toilet bowl was invented by Thomas Crapper. Dr. Nicholas taught us that when she visited our school."*

"How about Turdinator?" suggested Neil. "That doesn't have the word 'crapper' in it."

"I have an idea!" shouted Andrea. "Cushy Tushie!"

"That's a great idea, Andrea!" said Emily, who thinks all Andrea's ideas are great.

"Fanny Canny!" shouted Michael.

"Butt Hut!" shouted Ryan.

"Squat Spot!" shouted Neil.

---

* If you don't believe me, read *My Weirder School #8: Dr. Nicholas Is Ridiculous!*

"Hot Seat!" "Mr. Toilet!" "Royal Flush!" "Glow Bowl!" "Thunder Throne!" Everybody was shouting out names for the toilet seat.

Some of them were funny: Sir Flush-a-Lot. Poop-O-Matic. Mean Green Potty Machine. Some of them were just dumb. Like Fabulous Floater Flusher.

I wasn't coming up with any ideas. I thought and thought until my head hurt.

"How about you, A.J.?" asked Mr. Cooper. "Do you have any names for our toilet seat? You're usually good at this sort of thing."

"I don't have any ideas," I admitted.

"Arlo," said Andrea, "you are such a party pooper."

As soon as those words were out of her mouth, everything stopped. I looked at Andrea. Andrea looked at Emily. Emily looked at Neil. Neil looked at Ryan. Ryan looked at me. Time seemed to stand still for a moment. It was like the sky opened up, rainbows appeared, and angels started singing.

"Party Pooper!" I yelled. "We should call it Party Pooper! It's the perfect name!"

Everybody started shouting. "Yes!" "That's it!" "You're a genius!"

At that moment, the bell rang. It was three o'clock. Time to go home.

"Great!" said Mrs. Master. "We'll call it Party Pooper. I *love* it! I'll type up the business plan and print it out tonight.

Tomorrow we'll work on a prototype."

"Huh?" we all said.

"A prototype is a model of the finished product," said Mrs. Master.

"Leave it to me!" said Mr. Cooper. "This is a job for Cooperman!"

PARTY POOPER!

You Ain't Seen Nothin' Yet

The next morning, the weirdest thing in the history of the world happened. Mr. Cooper came running into the classroom.

Well, that's not the weird part. Mr. Cooper comes running into the classroom *every* morning. The weird part was that he came running into the classroom with a toilet seat over his head! You don't see *that* every day!

Mr. Cooper thinks he's a superhero. But he's not a very good one, because he tripped over somebody's backpack and almost slammed his head into his own desk.

"No worries," he said, jumping up off the floor. "I'm okay!"

At that moment, Mrs. Master rolled into the class on her hover board lawn mower.

"I see you finished the Party Pooper prototype," she said to Mr. Cooper.

"Yup!" he replied. "Isn't it a beauty? I made it with my own hands."

Big deal. It would be a lot harder to make a toilet seat with somebody else's hands.

We all gathered around to see the Party Pooper prototype. It *was* beautiful. I think it's safe to say it was the most beautiful toilet seat I had ever seen. And believe me, I've seen a lot of toilet seats in my time.

At that moment, Mr. Klutz came into the class. He was followed by a whole bunch of teachers—our librarian, Mrs. Roopy; the computer teacher, Mrs. Yonkers; the art teacher, Ms. Hannah; and the school counselor, Dr. Brad. Our class was swarming with teachers!

"We heard about your new toilet seat," Mr. Klutz said excitedly. "We wanted to see it."

"It looks like a plain old toilet seat to me," said Mrs. Roopy.

"Ah, but it's *different*," said Mrs. Master as she unrolled a cord attached to the toilet seat and plugged it into an electric outlet. "Here, touch it."

Mrs. Roopy put her hand on the toilet seat.

"Ooh, it's warm and toasty," she said.

"Hey," I shouted, "maybe people could use it to make toast!"

"Nobody's going to make toast on a toilet seat, dumbhead!" said Andrea.

"Oh, snap!" said Ryan.

I was going to say something mean to Andrea, but I didn't have the chance.

"Check this out," said Mr. Cooper. "Turn off the lights in the room, please."

Somebody flipped the switch. Everything went black except for the toilet seat, which gave off a soft blue light.

"It glows in the dark!" said Mrs. Master. "So you can find it at night without turning the lights on."

"Cool!" all the teachers yelled.

"And it smells nice too," added Mr. Cooper. "The heating element inside the toilet seat activates a floral scent. It will make

people feel like they're pooping in a fragrant forest."

Who wants to poop in the forest? I'd rather poop in a bathroom. I bet even bears would rather poop in a bathroom than in the forest.*

"It's amazing!" said Ms. Hannah.

"You ain't seen *nothin'* yet," said Mr. Cooper as he waved his hand in front of the toilet seat. "Listen to this."

"My . . . name . . . is . . . Party Pooper," the toilet seat said in a computery voice. "I'm . . . your . . . friend."

"Your toilet seat *talks*?" asked Dr. Brad.

---

* That is, if bears even knew that we *have* bathrooms, which they probably don't. It would be weird if bears knew that we had bathrooms.

"It does more than just talk," said Mr. Cooper. "I worked with our computer teacher, Mrs. Yonkers, on this part. We put a motion detector and a computer chip in Party Pooper. When it senses there's a person nearby, it will have a little conversation with you to keep you company while you're in the bathroom. Go ahead, try it."

"Hello, Party Pooper," said Mr. Klutz. "Nice weather we're having, isn't it?"

"Lovely," said the toilet seat. "Why . . . don't . . . you . . . sit . . . down? How . . . is . . . your . . . day . . . going?"

"It's a hard day," Mr. Klutz told the toilet seat.

"Tell . . . me . . . about . . . your . . . hard . . . day," said Party Pooper.

"Oh, I had another fight with Dr. Carbles, the president of the Board of Education," Mr. Klutz replied. "He doesn't like me very much."

"And . . . how . . . does . . . that . . . make . . . you . . . feel?" asked Party Pooper.

"Terrible," said Mr. Klutz.

"I . . . am . . . sorry . . . you . . . had . . . a . . . fight," said Party Pooper. "Perhaps . . . things . . . will . . . turn out . . . better . . . tomorrow."

"See?" said Mrs. Master. "The toilet seat uses artificial intelligence, so it sounds just like a real counselor."

50

"I feel better already!" said Mr. Klutz.

Dr. Brad, our school counselor, didn't look very happy.

"Wait a minute," he said. "So this thing can help you with your personal problems while you're in the bathroom?"

"That's right," said Mrs. Master.

Dr. Brad sighed and made his way toward the door.

"I guess you won't be needing *me* anymore," he said. "I figured I might lose my job someday. But I never thought I'd be replaced by a toilet seat."

My Genius Idea

We all felt bad for Dr. Brad. It would be a bummer to lose your job to a toilet seat. But the other teachers were really excited about Party Pooper.

"I want to buy one!" said Mrs. Roopy.

"Me too!" said Ms. Hannah.

"Me three!" said Mrs. Yonkers.

"We don't have any Party Poopers to sell yet," said Mrs. Master. "Before we can sell it, we need to raise some money."

"Why?" asked Mr. Cooper. "People are going to give us money when they buy the toilet seat, right?"

"Yes," said Mrs. Master, "but we have to get a factory to build more Party Poopers so we have something to sell. That costs money. You have to spend money to make money, and it costs a *lot* to create a new product. Toilet seats don't grow on trees, you know."

That would be cool if toilet seats *did* grow on trees. Of course, if toilet seats grew on trees, there would be no reason

to start a company to sell them. You could just pick them off the trees, like fruit.

Mrs. Master said we needed to make

a thousand toilet seats to start. Then, if sales were good, we would tell the factory to make another thousand.

A thousand toilet seats? That would cost a *lot* of money.

We all went through our pockets to see how much money we had. Ryan had a dollar. Emily had two quarters. I had thirty-five cents and some gummy bears. We didn't have nearly enough money to build a thousand toilet seats.

That's when I got *another* genius idea.

"Hey," I said, "in NASCAR they have stickers with company logos all over the cars. Like, Burger King will pay money so they can put their logo on the car. What if we did that with Party Pooper?"

"Burger King isn't going to put their logo on a toilet seat, dumbhead!" Andrea told me.

That's it. I was sick of Andrea saying mean things to me.

"Your *face* looks like a toilet seat," I shouted at her.

"Oh, snap!" said Ryan.

"Here's what we need to do," said Mrs. Master. "We need to get investors—grownups who will pay money to buy shares in our company. Then, if the company makes money, the investors will get some of the profits."

"Party Pooper can't miss," Mr. Cooper

said as he reached into his pocket. "I want to invest my life savings in the company. I'll chip in a thousand dollars."

"WOW," we all said, which is "MOM" upside down. A thousand is one less than a million!

Mr. Cooper wrote out a check and gave it to Mrs. Master.

"I'll invest a thousand dollars too!" said Mrs. Roopy. "I want to buy a piece of the company."

"Me too!" said Ms. Hannah.

"Me three!" said Mrs. Yonkers.

"Me four!" said Mr. Klutz.

All the teachers started writing checks and taking money out of their wallets to give to Mrs. Master. They were practically throwing checks and bills at her. I had never seen so much money in my life.

"This is fantastic!" Mrs. Master said as she counted the money. "I'll contact some factories this afternoon. Then they can start making Party Poopers right away."

"Of course the *children* will still own most of the shares in the company," said

Mrs. Master. "After all, Party Pooper was their idea."

"Yay!" we all shouted.

Everybody was excited about our new company. All the teachers were shaking hands and hugging each other. Mrs. Yonkers said she would set up a website so people could order Party Pooper over the internet. Ms. Hannah said she would make some artwork to use in newspapers and magazines, and online.

This thing was really happening! We were gonna make bazillions! And the whole thing was my idea.

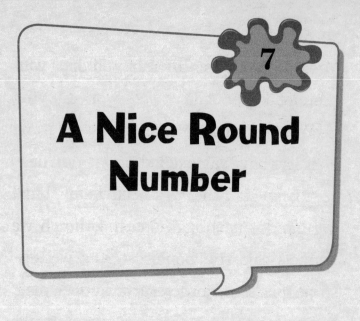

A Nice Round Number

7

"What are we going to study now?" Andrea asked Mr. Cooper after the other teachers left the classroom. "Reading, writing, or math?"

"None of those things," Mr. Cooper replied. "We're going talk about toilet seats."

Well *that* was different. I'll bet *your* teacher never said instead of studying reading, writing, or math, you were going to talk about toilet seats.

"The next thing we need to do," said Mrs. Master, "is to decide how much we charge for Party Pooper."

"Why don't we give it away for free?" suggested Emily. "That way, lots of people can enjoy it."

"Then we don't make any money, dumbhead," I told Emily. "You can't make money if you give stuff away for free!"

"You're mean!" Emily shouted, and then she went running out of the room.

Sheesh. What a crybaby.

"That wasn't very nice, A.J.," said Mrs. Master. "But you're right. You've got to charge money to make money."

"How about we sell it for ten dollars?" suggested Neil.

"Well, the factory will probably charge around fifty dollars just to *make* each Party Pooper," said Mrs. Master. "We would *lose* money if we sold it for ten dollars."

"How about we sell it for a hundred dollars?" Ryan suggested. "That's a nice round number."

"Hmmm," said Mrs. Master.

"So if we sell ten Party Poopers for a hundred dollars each," said Mr. Cooper, "how much money will come in?"

Everybody rushed to take a calculator out of their desk.

"A thousand dollars!" shouted Andrea. Then she smiled the smile that she smiles to let everybody know that she knows something nobody else knows.

"Right!" said Mr. Cooper. "And if we sell a *hundred* Party Poopers for a hundred dollars each, how much money will come in?"

Everybody rushed to figure it out.

"Ten thousand dollars!" shouted Andrea before anybody else.

"Right!" replied Mr. Cooper.

"Hey," I said. "I thought you told us we weren't going to work on math. This sounds a lot like math to me."

"Not at all, A.J.," said Mr. Cooper. "This isn't math. We're just talking about toilet seats. And if we sell a *thousand* Party Poopers for a hundred dollars each, how much money will come in?"

Everybody rushed to figure it out. This was *really* sounding like math to me.

"A hundred thousand dollars!" shouted Andrea.

"Right!" said Mr. Cooper. "And if we sell *ten thousand* Party Poopers for a hundred dollars each, how much money will come in?"

"A MILLION DOLLARS!" shouted Andrea.

"Right!"

"Hey, how many Party Poopers do we have to sell to make a bazillion dollars?" I asked.

"There's no such thing as a bazillion dollars," said Mrs. Master.

I *knew* it!

"A hundred dollars seems like a good price to me," said Alexia.

"I don't know," said Michael. "That still sounds like a lot of money to pay for a toilet seat."

"Here's a little secret," said Mrs. Master, lowering her voice to a whisper. "Instead of charging a hundred dollars, we can sell the Party Pooper for $99.99."

"But that's just one penny less than a hundred dollars," said Andrea.

"Yes, but it *sounds* like a lot less than a hundred dollars," said Mrs. Master. "That's why prices for things we buy often end with ninety-nine cents."

That didn't make any sense at all. Or cents.

"You are all shareholders in the

company," said Mrs. Master, "so you need to vote on it. All those in favor of selling Party Pooper for $99.99, say aye."

"Aye!" we all shouted.

"All those opposed, say nay."

Nobody said nay. I wasn't going to make horse noises.

"Then it's decided," said Mrs. Master. "We'll sell Party Pooper for $99.99."

Door-to-Door

When we got to school the next morning, it was just like any other day. Except that it was completely different.

Mr. Cooper was on the phone, yelling at somebody.

"I told you we need a thousand toilet seats!" he hollered. "And we need them *now*!"

While Mr. Cooper was arguing, Andrea had on her worried face.

"What's the matter with you?" I asked her. "Did your clog-dancing lesson get canceled?"

"No," she said. "I'm worried that Mr. Cooper is going overboard with this toilet seat thing."

"He's falling out of a boat?" I asked.

What do boats have to do with toilet seats? I didn't even see a boat anywhere.*

"No, dumbhead!" said Andrea. "Can't you see? Mr. Cooper doesn't pay any attention to teaching anymore. I asked him if we were going to work on our spelling

---

* How would they get a boat into our classroom in the first place?

today, and he said we would spend the whole day selling toilet seats!"

"Good," I told Andrea. "Why do we need to know how to spell if we can make bazillions selling Party Poopers?"

"Bazillions is *not* a real number, Arlo!" Andrea huffed.

I was going to say something mean to her, but that's when Mrs. Master came rolling into the class on her hover board lawn mower.

"Sorry I'm late," she said. "I was working on my next invention. It's a smoke detector that stops beeping when you shout 'I'm just cooking bacon!'"

"That's a great idea, Grandma!" said Alexia.

Mr. Cooper finished his phone call and told us the factory promised they would deliver five hundred toilet seats on Monday and another five hundred a few days later.

"Yay!" everybody shouted.

"Great!" said Mrs. Master. "Now it's time for us to tell the world about our new product. Word of mouth is the best advertising. So we're going to go out in the street selling Party Poopers door-to-door."

"Is Mr. Klutz okay with us doing this during school hours?" asked Emily.

"Sure he is!" said Mrs. Master. "He's a part owner of our company, remember?"

It was cool to leave school in the middle of the day. Mrs. Master and Mr. Cooper were the line leaders. We walked a million hundred miles until we got to a street with a bunch of houses on it.

"Okay," said Mrs. Master when we stopped at the first house. "You kids ring the doorbell and see if you can sell this family a Party Pooper."

We ran up the steps. Ryan rang the bell. I held the Party Pooper prototype. A lady came to the door.

"Do you want to buy a toilet seat?" we all yelled.

The lady screamed.

"Get out!" she hollered. Then she slammed the door in our faces. We all went running back down the steps.

That lady was mean. Mrs. Master told us not to be discouraged.

We walked to the next house, and this time we decided to just have *one* of us

make the sales pitch. Ryan rang the bell, and a man came to the door.

"Excuse me, sir," Ryan said. "Do you want to buy a toilet seat?"

"No thank you," the man replied.

"It's just $99.99," said Neil. "That's a penny less than a hundred dollars."

"I don't care how much it costs," the man replied. "I don't need a new toilet seat."

"Oh, okay."

We went back down the steps. At least that guy didn't yell at us.

"You're doing great," Mrs. Master told us when we got back to the sidewalk. "If at first you don't succeed, try, try again."

Andrea said she wanted a turn. We walked to the next house. Ryan rang the bell. A lady came to the door.

"Excuse me, ma'am, do you want to buy a toilet seat?" Andrea asked.

"I already have a toilet seat," the lady replied.

"Not like *this* one," Andrea told her. "It's heated, and it glows in the dark, so you can see it at night. And it talks. You can even have a conversation with it."

"My . . . name . . . is . . . Party Pooper," the toilet seat said. "I'm . . . your . . . friend."

"That's creepy," the lady said. "I don't want to have a conversation with my toilet seat."

"I . . . am . . . sorry . . . you . . . think . . .

I . . . am . . . creepy," said Party Pooper. "Perhaps . . . things . . . will . . . be . . . better . . . tomorrow."

"You can turn off the voice if you want to," Andrea told the lady.

"No thanks."

We all put on our best puppy dog faces, because that usually works when you want something from a grown-up.

"Please, please, please, please, *please*?" we all begged.

You can't miss when you put on a puppy dog face and say "Please, please, please, please, please."

"How much does it cost?" the lady asked.

"$99.99," we all said.

"A hundred bucks for a toilet seat?!" said the lady. "Forget it!"

She closed the door. Emily started crying, of course.

We went to a bunch of other houses after that. *Nobody* wanted to buy a Party Pooper. Bummer in the summer!

"Don't feel bad," Mrs. Master told us. "I've been rejected a million times."

It felt even longer walking the million hundred miles back to school. Mr. Klutz was waiting for us at the front door.

"So, how many toilet seats did you sell?" he asked. "A thousand?

"No," we replied.

"A hundred?"

"Not exactly."

"Well, how many did you sell?" asked Mr. Klutz.

"None," I admitted.

It was the worst day of my life.

Ding! Ding! Ding!

"What are we going to do *now*?" Ryan asked when we got back to class.

"Maybe I should cancel the order with the factory," said Mr. Cooper.

"Don't be silly!" said Mrs. Master. "This is just the beginning. We've got to give it more time."

"But if we can't sell the thousand toilet seats we ordered," said Mr. Cooper, "we'll lose our shirts!"

That made no sense at all. What do shirts have to do with toilet seats?

That's when I got the greatest idea in the history of the world.

Shirts made me think of people wearing shirts.

People wearing shirts made me think of *famous* people wearing shirts.

Famous people wearing shirts made me think of famous people wearing shirts while they're sitting on a toilet bowl.

"We should get some *celebrities* to say how much they like Party Pooper!" I shouted.

"That's not a bad idea!" said Mrs. Master. "When celebrities say they like something, everybody else wants to have it too."

Andrea looked mad because she didn't think of my great idea.

"Do you kids know any celebrities?" asked Mr. Cooper.

"What about Miss Suki?" suggested Neil. "She was that famous children's book author who visited our school."

"Children's book authors aren't famous," Michael replied.

"How about Mr. Hynde?" I suggested.

Mr. Hynde used to be our music teacher, but then he won that reality TV show where people sing and dance. Now he's a famous rapper.

"That's a *great* idea, A.J.!" said Mr. Cooper. "I love it."

I'm full of great ideas. I stuck out my tongue at Andrea to let her know that I came up with the great idea and she didn't. Nah-nah-nah boo-boo on her.

"Do you think Mr. Hynde would do a rap for us?" asked Ryan. "We could film it and put it on the internet."

"There's only one way to find out," Mr. Cooper said as he took out his cell phone. "I'll call him."

And you'll never believe who walked into the door a few minutes later.

Nobody! It would hurt if you walked into a door. I thought we went over that in chapter 3. But you'll never believe who walked into the door*way*.

It was Mr. Hynde!

"Yo, my homies!" he said as we all ran over to hug him. Then he shook hands with Mr. Cooper and Mrs. Master. They showed him the Party Pooper prototype.

"So let me get this straight," said Mr. Hynde. "You want me to rap about this toilet seat?"

"Yeah!" we all shouted.

"And it's heated?" he asked.

"Yeah!"

"And it glows in the dark?"

"Yeah!"

"And it's scented?"

"Yeah!"

"And it talks?"

"Yeah!"

"Hmmmm," Mr. Hynde said, thinking it over for a few seconds. "Okay, I've got it. Somebody give me a beat."

Mr. Cooper started beat boxing. Mrs. Master pointed her cell phone at Mr. Hynde. And he started rapping. . . .

"How can you pee when you cannot see?
That's what folks keep asking me.
Pooping gets old
when your seat's too cold.
At least that's what I have been told.

"You want it heated while you are seated.
You want it hot when you're on the pot.
You want it lit up while you sit up.
You want that glow when you gotta go.

"That's why you need Party Pooper.
I said, Party Pooper! Party Pooper!

"The Party Pooper is super-duper,
like Mrs. Master and Mr. Cooper.

"This toilet seat is very fine,
and it only costs
ninety-nine ninety-nine.

"The best part about this toilet is
you'll never have to oil it, kids.

"So get rid of your seat.
It can't compete
with the coolest toilet
out on the street.

"And it smells so sweet.
Send out a tweet.

You'll get a receipt.
Let me repeat.

"It's really neat.
The hottest seat
out on the street
is Party Pooper. . . ."

When he was done, everybody clapped and cheered.

"Great!" said Mrs. Master. "Okay, let's upload the video to YouTube."

Mr. Cooper and Mrs. Master added a link to the website so people could order Party Poopers right after watching the video.

"Now all we can do is wait," said Mr. Cooper.

We didn't have to wait long. After a few seconds, there was a sound.

Ding!

We all looked at the computer screen.

"Look! We just sold our first toilet seat!" shouted Alexia. "We did it!"

"Yay!" everybody shouted.

Ding!

"That's *another* one!" shouted Andrea.

Ding! Ding! Ding! Ding!

"Four more!" shouted Neil.

Ding! Ding! Ding! Ding! Ding! Ding! Ding! Ding! Ding! Ding! Ding! Ding!

"Party Poopers are selling like crazy!" hollered Mrs. Masters. "I've never seen a product sell so fast!"

Ding! Ding! Ding! Ding! Ding! Ding!
Ding! Ding! Ding! Ding! Ding! Ding!

"We're going to be rich!" shouted Alexia.

Ding! Ding! Ding! Ding! Ding!

"We're going to be millionaires!" shouted Michael.

Ding! Ding! Ding! Ding! Ding!

"Billionaires!" shouted Ryan.

Ding! Ding! Ding! Ding! Ding!

"Bazillionaires!" I shouted.

It was the greatest day of my life.

10

Mrs. Master Is a Disaster!

You should have *been* there! Sales of Party Poopers were going through the roof!

Well, not really. If that happened, we'd have to get a new roof.

But sales were *really* good. The first five hundred toilet seats arrived the next day, and we spent the whole morning shipping them out to customers all over the world.

On the website, people were already posting messages saying how much they loved their Party Poopers.

"When will we get our money?" I asked Mrs. Masters.

"In a few days," she told me. "Be patient."

A few days later, I looked out the window during math and saw a truck pull up to the school.

"That must be our money!" I shouted. "We earned so many bazillions of dollars, they have to bring it in a truck!"

"We're rich!" yelled Ryan.

We all watched out the window as a big guy wearing overalls unloaded a bunch of boxes from the truck.

"What are you going to do with your bazillions?" Neil asked me.

"I'm going to buy every video game in the world," I said.

"I'm going to buy every candy bar in the world," said Ryan.

"I'm going to take a trip around the world," said Alexia.

"I'm so excited!" said Andrea, rubbing her hands together.

After a million hundred minutes, the guy from the truck came into our class rolling the boxes of money.

"Thanks for delivering our money," said Mr. Cooper, rubbing his hands together.

"Oh, this isn't money," the guy replied. "It's five hundred toilet seats."

"Oh," we all said, disappointed.

"Where do you want me to put 'em?" the guy asked.

"You can stack them in the corner there," said Mr. Cooper.

Mrs. Master rolled in on her hover board lawn mower.

"I have great news!" she announced. "We sold *another* five hundred Party Poopers last night! I already placed an order at the factory to make a thousand more!"

"Yay!"

"We're rich!" I shouted. "I'll never have

to go to school again."

"Me neither!" said Mr. Cooper. "I'm going to retire. Who needs to teach? I'm going to live off my toilet seat income."

Suddenly, Mr. Klutz came running into the class. He was all out of breath, and he looked upset.

"What's the matter?" asked Mrs. Master.

"It's all over the news!" shouted Mr. Klutz. "One of our toilet seats caught on fire!"

"WHAT?!" we all shouted.

"It was in Ohio!" Mr. Klutz said. "A man was sitting on his Party Pooper when it caught on fire! Something must have been wrong with the heater! He got burned on his butt!"

"Gasp!" we all gasped.

"He says he's going to sue us for a hundred million dollars!" shouted Mr. Klutz.

"Oh no!" we all hollered.

Mr. Cooper ran over to the computer to check the website.

Ding! Ding! Ding! Ding! Ding! Ding! Ding! Ding! Ding! Ding! Ding! Ding! Ding! Ding! Ding! Ding! Ding!

"Emails are pouring in!" shouted Mr. Cooper.

"What do they say?" asked Mr. Klutz.

"Everybody wants their money back!" shouted Mr. Cooper. "What are we going to do *now*?"

"We have to give them their money

back," said Mrs. Master. "We sold them a defective product."

"Nobody's going to buy Party Poopers if they cause butt burns!" shouted Mr. Cooper.

"What are we going to do with the

thousand toilet seats you ordered?" shouted Mr. Klutz.

Everybody started yelling and screaming and shrieking and hooting and hollering and freaking out.

"It's all over," groaned Mr. Cooper, holding his head in his hands. "I put my life savings into Party Pooper. And now I'm going to lose my shirt!"

Mr. Cooper must lose a lot of shirts or he wouldn't be talking about losing them all the time.

"This is *your* fault, Arlo!" Andrea yelled. "Party Pooper was *your* idea!"

Everybody was looking at me. This was the worst day of my life. I wanted to go to Antarctica and live with the penguins.

They don't use toilet seats.

But there was no way I was going to take all the blame for what happened.

"It wasn't *my* fault," I said. "It was Mrs. Master's fault! *She's* the one who showed us how to start our own company."

Everybody in the class turned to look at Mrs. Master.

"Well, this has been a lot of fun, you guys," she said. "But I have to go now. I need to work on my next invention: a solar-powered backscratcher."

She hustled out of the class like she had to catch a bus.

Oh, well, I guess we're not going to make bazillions after all. Maybe I'll get to see *Star Wars*. Maybe Grandpa Bert will stop making armpit noises. Maybe a truck full of toilet seats will fall on Andrea's head. Maybe bears will figure out that we have bathrooms and stop pooping in the forest. Maybe Mr. Cooper will fall out of a boat. Maybe people will start making toast on their toilet seats. Maybe Dr. Brad will get his job back. Maybe I'll plant a toilet seat tree in our backyard. Maybe Mr. Cooper will find all those shirts he lost. Maybe Burger King will put their logo on a toilet seat. Maybe we'll have to get a new roof. Maybe we'll think of a way to get rid of a thousand toilet seats. Maybe we'll figure out how to spell what Mr. Klutz is. Maybe we can train penguins to start using toilet seats.

But it won't be easy!*

---

* So did you like the story? If you liked it, tell your friends. And if you didn't like it, tell your friends you liked it.